First published in the UK in 2019
by New Frontier Publishing Europe Ltd
Uncommon, 126 New King's Rd, Fulham, London SW6 4LZ
www.newfrontierpublishing.co.uk

ISBN: 978-1-912858-12-5

A CIP catalogue record for this book
is available from the British Library.

Designed by Verity Clark

Printed in China
10 9 8 7 6 5 4 3 2 1

A Home for Luna

For Oscar and Nic.
With you, I am home.
~ S G

For Oscar and Willow.
~ M A

A Home for Luna

Stef Gemmill   Mel Armstrong

NEW FRONTIER PUBLISHING

On a moonlit night, a strange
shape washed ashore.

Luna placed one paw, then another,
onto the icy brown rocks. Her wet,
black fur stood up in spikes.

Luna licked her paws and wiped her ears.
She listened for the sounds of danger that
had made her leave her home. But she only
heard the *whoosh* of the waves.

Luna sheltered under the crate and dreamed of a home from long ago.

As daylight peeped
over the cliffs,

the cat woke.

She stretched.

A smell filled the air.

A smell like home,
but not exactly.

Luna tiptoed down the slippery rocks, sniffing the air.

On the beach sat rows and rows of tall black-and-white birds with pointy red beaks.

Each penguin gobbled salty, sweet sardines. Luna's stomach groaned.

The penguins huddled closer as Luna watched. One tall penguin with large yellow eyes stood alone.

Yellow-Eye blinked at Luna. Luna blinked back.
She crouched close to the rock. Her legs could
not take one more step.

As the morning light grew brighter,
the larger penguins slid into the ocean,
returning with mouths full of fish.

Luna licked her lips. Still tired,
she napped on the warm rocks.

When Luna woke, a tiny penguin waddled closer, watched by Yellow-Eye.

Tiny rolled a spiral-shaped shell over the sand towards Luna.

Luna rolled it back.

Tiny danced on her little webbed feet.
She pulled the shellfish from its shell
and rolled it along the sand.

Luna gulped it down and purred.

On the next moonlit night, Luna caught fish with the penguins. Not exactly like a penguin . . . but good enough.

When gulls tried to steal her catch,
Luna pounced at their pecking beaks.

Yellow-Eye jumped and snapped at the gulls.
Not exactly like a cat . . . but good enough.

Each day Luna moved
closer to Yellow-Eye.

Soon she joined the huddle
just like the other penguins.

On the next moonless night, a strange
boat scraped onto the shore.

Shouts echoed across the beach.

The penguins huddled closer together.

'This is no place for a cat.' said the fisherman.
'Eee-oww!' howled Luna.

The penguins pecked at the man.
Luna hissed and scratched, wriggling free.

Yellow-Eye and the penguins closed around Luna.

Together they watched the light
of the boat fade into the darkness.

Luna purred. Here, with the penguins, she'd found her home.